The Emperor Who Forgot His Birthday

For Rona

Barefoot Beginners
an imprint of
Barefoot Books
37 West 17th Street
4th Floor East
New York, New York, 10010

This book is printed on 100% acid-free paper

This book was typeset in Perpetua
The illustrations were prepared in pen and watercolor on 140lb watercolor paper

Graphic design by Design Principals, England
Color separation by Grafiscan, Italy
Printed and bound in Singapore by Tien Wah Press (Pte) Ltd.

1 3 5 7 9 8 6 4 2

Publisher Cataloging-in-Publication Data

Edmiston, Jim.
    The Emperor who forgot his birthday / written and illustrated
by Jim Edmiston—1st ed.
[32]p. : col. ill. ;   cm.
Summary: Count the letters, cakes and toys that the Emperor's
servants are taking to the palace for a birthday surprise, and find
Saffron and Mustard the cat, concealed in the page.
ISBN 1-84148-015-0
1. Birthdays—Fiction—Juvenile literature. 2. Counting— Juvenile
literature. I. Title.
  [E]—dc21 1999 AC CIP

The Emperor Who Forgot His Birthday

Written and illustrated by Jim Edmiston

BAREFOOT BOOKS

The Emperor with the longest beard in the world was usually a happy, smiling Emperor. But one morning he woke up to find that his cat, Mustard, was not lying purring beside him.

And there were no servants to help him get dressed. "Emperors don't put their slippers on all by themselves," he grumbled, as he squeezed them onto the wrong feet.

Every morning, the Emperor had breakfast with his granddaughter, Saffron, but today there was no sign of her. "An emperor doesn't make his own breakfast," he complained.

He had never made breakfast before. He looked for the cornflakes, but he couldn't find them anywhere. So he got a big bowl and filled it with beets, jam, baked beans, strawberries, and old fish. It tasted horrible.

"Where are all my servants?" cried the Emperor, looking in the broom closet and behind the couch. "This isn't their day off! What are they up to? Where is everybody?"

The Emperor was very puzzled. He did not realize that his servants were busy tiptoeing into the palace with lots of presents for him. How many can you see?

"Where is Saffron?" cried the Emperor. "And where is Mustard, the yellowest cat in the world?" He went right to the top of the palace and searched all over the playroom.

The Emperor looked in the dolls' house. He looked on the bookshelves. He looked behind the building blocks. He was so busy that he did not notice any of the birthday balloons. How many can you see?

The Emperor had forgotten his own birthday! He scratched his head and tweaked his long beard. He closed his eyes and thought hard. He drummed his fingers on his fat, round tummy and pulled his ears.

"Is it Monday or Tuesday or Wednesday or Thursday or Friday or Saturday or Sunday?" he wondered. But he could not remember. Behind him, Mustard and Saffron giggled, but he did not hear them.

The Emperor decided to cheer himself up. With his slippers pointing the wrong way, and just one mouthful of horrid breakfast inside his tummy, he stamped his feet, slammed the palace door, and stomped off into town.

The Emperor was determined to have fun. But Saffron and Mustard were watching. They tiptoed behind him to make sure that he was home in time for his big birthday surprise.

Outside the bakery, the Emperor cried, "Give me poundcakes, chocolate cake, fruitcake, date and walnut cake, and those fancy marzipanny ones with cherries all over them!"

"I am sorry, Your Highness," said the baker. "There are no cakes left. They have all been sold." The Emperor felt even hungrier. He did not notice all the cakes being carried to the palace. How many can you see?

At the toy store, the Emperor shouted, "Bring me a yo-yo, a spinning top, a teddy bear, a Noah's ark, a rocking horse, and one of those rainbow-colored, whiz-bang, monster, rubbery, hoopla, robot things!"

"I am sorry, Your Highness," said the toymaker. "There are no toys left. They have all been sold." The Emperor was so disappointed that he did not notice all the toys being carried to the palace. How many can you see?

In front of the candy store, the Emperor cheered up. "Give me chocolate bars, jawbreakers, chewy taffy, and bags and bags of minty, malty, melty, mouth-watering, munchy candy!"

"I am sorry, Your Highness," said the owner. "There is no candy left. It has all been sold." The Emperor was so sad that he did not notice the trays of candy being carried to the palace. How many can you see?

"No cakes! No toys! No candy!" moaned the droopy old Emperor.
"Perhaps the clowns will make me laugh with their joking and juggling
and red noses and honking horns and buckets of glittering stars."

"I am sorry, Your Highness," said the town jester. "The clowns are not here today." The Emperor was too fed up to notice all of the clowns wending their way to the palace. How many can you see?

The Emperor slumped down outside the magician's tent. "It would be so nice," he said quietly, "to see just one of those hey-presto, open-sesame, hocus-pocus, abracadabra, disappearing-rabbit-in-a-hat tricks."

But the magician was scampering off to the palace with all his white rabbits. How many can you see?

Then the magician's assistant stepped out from her tent. "I have just one trick left," she said. Quick as a flash, she shook her magic cloak

and tossed it over the Emperor. As he spun around and around, the Emperor started to remember why today was a special day.

When the cloak was pulled away, the Emperor opened his eyes.
He found himself in the grandest room in the palace.
"Yes, yes, yes!" he cried excitedly. "Now I remember what day it is."

"Happy Birthday!" sang the baker, the toymaker, the candy storeowner, the clowns and the magician.

Soon the sad, grumpy, droopy Emperor became the happiest Emperor he had ever been. And when all the hip-hip-hoorays were over, and everyone

had finished playing silly games with marzipan cakes, whirligigs, and chewy taffy, Saffron told the story of the Emperor who forgot his birthday.

BAREFOOT BOOKS publishes high-quality picture books for
children of all ages and specializes in the work of artists and writers from
many cultures. If you have enjoyed this book and would like to receive a copy of
our current catalog, please contact our New York office —
Barefoot Books Inc., 37 West 17th Street, 4th Floor East, New York, New York, 10010
e-mail: ussales@barefoot-books.com   website: www.barefoot-books.com